THE GHOST OF
TUTANKHAMUN

Also by Steve Cole:

THE GHOST OF TUTANKHAMUN

STEVE COLE

Illustrated by Donough O'Malley

RED FOX

RED FOX

UK | USA | Canada | Ireland | Australia
India | New Zealand | South Africa

Red Fox is part of the Penguin Random House group of companies
whose addresses can be found at global.penguinrandomhouse.com.

www.penguin.co.uk
www.puffin.co.uk
www.ladybird.co.uk

Penguin
Random House
UK

First published 2016

001

Text copyright © Steve Cole, 2016
Logo artwork copyright © Andy Parker, 2014
Cover artwork copyright © Dave Shelton, 2016
Interior illustrations copyright © Donough O'Malley, 2016
Ancient Egypt Adviser – Louise Ellis-Barrett

The moral right of the author and illustrator has been asserted

Set in Bembo MT Schoolbook
Printed in Great Britain by Clays Ltd, St Ives plc

A CIP catalogue record for this book is available from the
British Library

ISBN: 978–0–849–41872–0

All correspondence to:
Red Fox
Penguin Random House Children's
80 Strand, London WC2R 0RL

MIX
Paper from
responsible sources
FSC
www.fsc.org   FSC® C018179

Penguin Random House is committed
to a sustainable future for our business,
our readers and our planet. This book
is made from Forest Stewardship Council®
certified paper.

For Amy

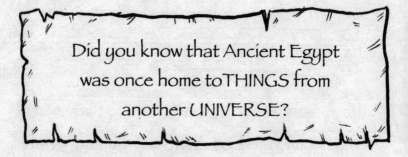

Did you know that Ancient Egypt was once home to THINGS from another UNIVERSE?

These MYSTERIOUS visitors from the realm of KaBa inspired the old Egyptians, who treated them like gods. But EVIL, BAD, FREAKY CREATURES also came to stay – so BIONIC SECRET AGENTS from KaBa were sent to catch them.

Thousands of years later, ONE of those secret agents is STILL on the case. Because SPOOKY MONSTERS remain on the loose . . .

In these pages you will meet:

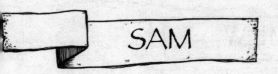

SAM

Brave, bold – but not very bright, Sam is the only Secret Agent Mummy still fighting crime all over our world. His supertough bandages protect him from enemy attacks and the passing years – he is thousands of years old! He lives in a portable Pyra-Base, hidden from human eyes. With magic, might, cool in-built weapons and a LOT of good luck, he blunders through adventures with the help of his friends . . .

MEW

This snooty cat goddess is the brains of Sam's outfit. She stayed on Earth because she loves the taste of fish! Annoying and vain, she will only help out on anti-bad-guy operations in exchange for worship and cod.

MUMBUM

This semi-robotic dog was once Sam's loyal hunting hound, until he met with a terrible accident. Only his bottom survived. Now wrapped in bandages, Mumbum can be strapped into different metal bodies for different situations – the ultimate utility pooch.

NIALL RIVERS

One fateful day, Niall found a magical relic from KaBa, touched it – and absorbed its powers! As a result, Niall is the only human able to see Sam's secret world. He has become Sam's special sidekick, helping him on his mad mummy adventures. Quick-thinking, courageous and good with gadgets – both those from Earth and those from KaBa – Niall shares Sam's mission to protect the world from incredible dangers.

NOW, LET THE ADVENTURE BEGIN . . .

Chapter One

Up Against It

The aliens closed in on Niall Rivers. Gruesome and green, their eyes swivelled on thick stalks, fixing him with a dozen merciless stares.

"Just one chance," Niall told himself, ducking and dodging as death rays zapped all around him. "I can fight my way through if I'm fast enough. If I concentrate really hard—"

"Niall!" An ear-exploding shriek erupted

behind him. "Mum says you've got to let me play *Princess Pony Parlour* NOW!"

"Wha—?" Niall jumped in surprise, and the controller slipped to the carpet. On the screen, the aliens laughed as they unleashed their lasers. The picture dissolved in glowing pixels.

GAME OVER!

"Nice work, Snitch." Niall glared at his little sister, Ellie (although "little" did not apply to her super-massive mega-mouth). "I was totally going to complete that level, and now you got me killed – just so you can play *Princess Poopy-Pants*!"

"Mum! Mum! Niall called my game something rude and he won't let me play it!" Ellie smiled at him and crossed her arms. "Prepare for payback, big brother!" she whispered.

"Snitch, you drive me crazy!" Niall groaned. He threw a cushion at her head – just as Mum came in.

Mum was looking tired and cross. "Honestly, you two! Why can't you ever just play nicely?"

"I'm not sure," said Niall thoughtfully. "Maybe because Ellie's a gigantic pain in the butt?"

"WAHHHH!" Ellie faked some pathetic sobs.

"Oh, Niall!" Mum scowled. "Your sister only wants a little go on her favourite game. Would it kill you to share?"

"I don't want to find out! But . . ." With a sigh, Niall tossed the controller to Ellie. "There. Have it. I'm going into the garden."

To be accurate, he thought, *the garden of the house next door.*

Niall smiled as he headed out through the back door. He was the keeper of the biggest secret in the whole world.

These days, he lived next door to a real-life, way-out, extra-bandaged superhero called Sam.

S-A-M – short for Secret Agent Mummy!

Niall quickly climbed the fence into next door's overgrown garden. Sam had parked his portable Pyra-Base here a few months back, while investigating a crazy criminal in the area.

That was how Niall had been dragged into the whole bonkers adventure in the first place . . .

"Hello? Sam!" Niall knocked on the great sandstone door of the Pyra-Base. It was an awe-inspiring sight, like an old Egyptian pyramid made weirdly modern with triangular windows and a chimney pot. "Anyone at home?"

There was no answer, so Niall put his ear to the door – and frowned. He could hear roars and snarls, like there were tigers inside. Tigers . . . or something worse.

6

"Sam?" Niall banged harder. "Sam! It's me, Niall. Are you—?"

"Come in, my friend!" came Sam's warm, familiar voice. "I will *not* not be short."

Niall opened the door. "You mean, you won't be *long*?"

"This is what I say!"

The roaring sound got louder as Niall stepped into the large, shady hallway with its built-in fig tree and Egyptian art on the walls. Nervously Niall turned right towards the operations room – the nerve centre of Secret Agent Mummy's 3,000-year crusade

against the criminals of KaBa.

He gasped. The operations room had gone! In its place stood a dark, circular enclosure, like the bottom of a pit. Two huge fleshy beasts, each with the body of a lion and a vast, scary human head, prowled over the dirty ground.

"Sphinxes!" Niall breathed. "But they're not made of stone, they're REAL!"

As the massive, muscular monsters moved apart, they revealed a bandaged figure in a hat and raincoat facing up to them with an ebony sword. "So, vile sphinxes! You want a piece of me, yes?" the figure cried. "Step up and taste

bandage. Cursed be your powerful paws and undeveloped noses!"

"Sam!" Niall shouted. "Stop talking to them and run!"

"Do not worry about me, my friend— OOOF!" Sam broke off as a huge sphinx paw

9

came down and flattened him. The other beast reared up to crush him underfoot.

"NO!" Niall hollered. "Leave Sam alone!"

The sphinxes ignored him. Niall ran up to them, waving his arms; he was terrified, but he *had* to try and lure the monsters away from his friend.

Finally his tactics seemed to work. With a roar, one of the huge sphinxes turned – and thundered towards him.

Niall had no time to run, no time to jump clear.

The sphinx was going to crush him!

Chapter Two

The K-Casket

Niall closed his eyes and yelled, waiting for the deadly impact ...

But the sphinx didn't hit him. It went straight *through* him, like a ghost!

"Ugh!" Niall cried. "That was horrible. What happened, Sam . . . ?"

The same sphinx found Sam a lot more solid – it turned and squashed him under its paws!

"Noooooooo!" yelled Niall.

As he did so, the whole scene faded away to darkness. The pit was gone – and in its place was the *real* operations room, the one Niall knew, the Pyra-Base's candle-lit control centre. The walls were covered with maps, charts and triangular TV screens. Four large jars, each with a lid shaped like the head of an animal, sat in alcoves. Normally a pyramid-shaped table stood in the middle of the room, but today everything had been cleared away to leave a space.

And there, lying on the floor, was Sam – totally unharmed!

"Forgive me, my friend!" He grinned. "I just wished to finish my game. To be back in KaBa – well, it was such a delight!"

"Right. A delight . . ." Niall said slowly. "That was just a *game*? It all seemed so real!"

"The sphinxes and their pit were only projections," Sam explained, getting up.

"But they clobbered you," said Niall. "How come they went straight through me?"

"Because you were not wearing one of *these*." Sam held up
his bandaged wrist to show
a thick gold bracelet studded
with buttons that sparkled like
red jewels. "It is a KaBangle. You
cannot play without it."

Niall studied it. "Like a controller, you mean?"

14

"The KaBangle makes you part of the projection, so you can join the games and activities stored inside *this*." Sam patted a pyramid-shaped silver case, no bigger than a shoebox, sitting on top of the table. "Behold the K-Casket."

"K?" Niall echoed.

"Yes, I am quite OK, thank you, my friend!" said Sam.

Niall took a deep, calming breath. "Is this K-Casket thing a kind of video-game console?"

"It is very much more than that, boy! MEEOWWWW!" A white cat, half wrapped in gold bandages, and with a wonky tiara on her

head, strutted over. "Yes, much, much more!"

"What do you mean?"

"Before I tell you . . . make me an offering of cod." Mew looked like a cat, but claimed to be a cat *goddess*. Like Sam, she had come to Earth from KaBa. Unlike Sam, she was a snooty know-all who expected a constant supply of fish and worship from everyone around her.

Niall patted his pockets. "I'm fresh out of fresh fish. Sorry."

"I have some!" Sam pulled a halibut from his back pocket. "Please, Great Mew, explain to our young friend."

16

Mew grabbed the fish, gave it a kiss, threw it in the air and swallowed it whole. "*Nom nom nom.* Very well!" She wiped her mouth with a dainty paw. "The K-Casket was not loaded with mere games. They were more like training exercises."

"What did that game you were playing train you for, Sam?" asked Niall. "How to get totally splatted?"

"How to be a sphinx pit cleaner. A most

important job back in KaBa." Sam sighed. "In truth, it makes me very sick of the home."

"*Homesick*, you mean?"

Sam nodded. "It is centuries since I saw my old home. To feel like I was back there . . ." He smiled. "It was a great boon to my mummified heart."

"Well, anyway!" Mew said briskly. "In exchange for leading their people in the worship of beings from KaBa, the pharaohs were given special perks."

"They got Secret Agent Mummies as bodyguards!" Sam cried.

"And they were also allowed to play on the K-Casket," Mew revealed. "The device seems wondrous even to your modern eyes – imagine how the ancient pharaohs must have boggled!"

Niall nodded slowly. He knew that KaBa's technology was a mixture of science and magic, and guessed that the K-Casket was powered by a large amount of both. Ancient it might be, but it was still super-advanced by human standards.

"The K-Casket did not only offer pharaohs experience in the ways of KaBa," Mew went on. "It gave them training for sports and activities in their Earthly world too, so they could

make themselves mightier than the humans they ruled."

"This one was given to the boy king, Tutankhamun, in 1330 BC!" Sam declared. "I found it in the Pyra-Base's garage while I was spring cleaning."

"Wait a sec." Niall was amazed. "This K-Casket thing actually belonged to *King Tut*?"

"Indeed this is so." Sam beamed. "You have been hearing of him?"

"Tutankhamun is, like, one of the most famous pharaohs ever!"

"Horus knows why!" Mew tutted. "The brat

did very little when he was Pharaoh. His advisers did all the real work – while he enjoyed himself on the K-Casket!"

"Ah, how young Tutankhamun loved the *Chariot Dash* training game!" said Sam. "He had a bad foot and used a crutch, so could not race chariots for real. But he loved to pretend."

"You've got a chariot simulation on that thing?" Niall asked eagerly. "I love races! Can I have a go?"

"You dare to ask such a thing?!" Mew looked shocked. "This is no mere screen game of the sort you humans spend your lives glued

to. This is a sacred tool of knowledge, boy! A precious relic that has enhanced the minds of the greatest kings and queens of Ancient Egypt! You are not worthy to explore its—"

"I'll give you a haddock later tonight," Niall tried.

"Oooooh! Then of course you can have a go!" Mew swiped Sam's KaBangle and tossed it to Niall. "Only, make sure it's a *juicy* haddock!"

You'll be getting fish fingers, thought Niall privately as he stepped up to the gleaming K-Casket. "How does it work?"

"The instructions are broadcast into your brain," said Mew. "That's why Sam did so badly catching sphinxes – the instructions had nowhere to go!"

Before Niall could turn it on, a black mechanical dog came flying into the operations room on four fiery paws, spewing jets of smoke and flame. He woofed happily – but the sound came from a bandaged bum with

a wagging tail, sticking out of the back of the robotic suit.

Niall smiled. "Hey, Mumbum!"

"*Arf,*" the robo-dog replied.

He looked like something from a video game himself. Long ago, Mumbum had been Sam's valiant dog – until an accident left him no more than a "mummy-bummy". Even so, once strapped into one of the many robotic bodies that had been made for him, Mumbum could still help his master in all sorts of ways. Right now he had an oilcan built into his nose and several screwdrivers sticking out of his collar.

"Behold the Mechanic-Mutt suit." Sam grinned. "I found something else in the garage, you see. A most exciting machine! Mumbum is helping me to fix it down."

"You mean, fix it *up*. Hey, could I help too?" Niall had always been good with gadgets. "I like the sound of an exciting machine!"

"Ah! I am sorry, Niall." Sam shook his head. "I wish for this to be the big surprise to you. A secret project!" The robo-dog yapped at him loudly. "For now, it seems there is a problem with it. Excuse me . . ." Sam bowed down to Mew and waved farewell to Niall.

"Now, then, boy." Mew's paw hovered over a button on the side of the K-Casket. "Are you ready to become the first human since ancient times to enter this incredible virtual world?"

"Er . . ."

"Good. Bye, then."

Mew pressed the button, and in an instant the operations room seemed to disappear into darkness. The KaBangle on Niall's wrist pulsed with golden energy.

"Welcome to the K-Casket learning realm," said a voice in his head. "Please choose an option from the main menu."

26

White hieroglyphs shone before his eyes. Niall immediately knew how to read them; it was one of many powers he had accidentally absorbed since Sam had moved in next door. "*KaBa Menu*," he read aloud. "*A Tour of KaBa, Launch a Sky-Boat, Train the Sphinxes—*"

"Stop," commanded a boy's voice. "Change to *Egypt Menu*."

Niall looked around in surprise to see who had spoken. Apart from the scrolling hieroglyphs, he couldn't see a thing. "*How to Lead*

an Army into Battle, Ride a Camel While Looking Cool, Irrigating Deserts the Easy Way—"

"*I* shall choose what we do here," the voice rang out.

"Er . . . who are you?" called Niall nervously.

He gasped as a ghostly figure appeared before him. It was a skinny teenage boy carrying a spear. He wore a white hat with a cobra pinned to the front of it, and a long black-and-gold tunic with a bright sash tied around the middle. There was a challenge in his dark, black-ringed eyes.

"I didn't know this thing came with

multi-player options." Niall raised his eyebrows. "Who are you?"

"I am the mighty pharaoh Tutankhamun!"
The boy raised his spear. "Now, are you going
to play my games or not?"

Chapter Three

The Race Is On

Niall stared at the figure before him. "But . . . you can't be Tutankhamun!"

Tut frowned. "I totally *am* him!"

"But . . . Tutankhamun died thousands of years ago!" Niall looked at the boy's feet. "And he used a crutch."

"Maybe the ORIGINAL did . . . but I'm King Tut the way he WISHED he could be!" Tut

grinned suddenly, showing large yellow teeth. "I'm faster, smarter, and not bossed around by boring grown-ups the whole time."

"Cool." Niall thought he understood. "On my console I have a kind of 'cartoon me' who links all my games and online stuff together. An *avatar*. I guess that's what Tut did too – only thanks to KaBa tech, you're an avatar with a mind of your own!"

"Your words are strange," Tut complained. "But if you mean I basically rule this K-Casket's virtual world, then you're right! Now, who are you, stranger?"

"Um, Niall."

"Well, Um-Niall, I don't know where you're from or why you're dressed like a weirdo, but come on – let's race chariots! I haven't raced anyone in an age!"

In quite a few ages, thought Niall. "Yeah, OK! I thought I'd be having a one-player game like my friend, but—"

"Hey, is that who woke me up? It was dark for so long, but then the lights came on and I heard sphinxes roaring in the pit . . ."

Niall considered. "Yes, that must be when Sam turned on the K-Casket and started playing."

"Who?"

"Sam," Niall repeated. "Secret Agent Mummy."

"YOU CALLED?" In a flash, Sam appeared! "Greetings, Niall! Since Mew did not tell you how to *stop* the game, I thought I had better get the second KaBangle and join you—" He saw the boy king and gasped. "Highness! Great Tutankhamun, can it be you?"

"Hey, it's one of those mummy things from KaBa, sent to guard and worship me!" King Tut punched the

33

air. "Goody, goody! More people to play against!"

Sam bowed politely. "Er, well, actually, it is time we must go—"

"*Go?* You can't *go*!" King Tut frowned and waved his spear. "I command you to stay!"

"Yeah, come on, Sam," said Niall. "We can give him a race."

Sam lowered his voice. "But Great Mew wiped the memory of this K-Casket. She did a reshoe."

"Reboot," Niall corrected him. "Well, she can't have done it right, dumb cat, because

Tut's video-game self – his avatar – is still here, isn't it?"

Sam nodded gravely. "Haunting the console like . . . a ghost!"

"Come on then," Tut cried. "I'll totally beat you!"

"But we haven't played before," Niall objected. "Can we have a practice?"

"Borrrrring!" Tut moaned. "All right, take the practice level on . . . *Chariot Dash*!"

As he called out the words, the main menu disappeared, and Niall felt dizzy, as if he was flying through space . . .

Then the darkness was sucked away, and Niall jumped to find himself in the middle of a gigantic oval racetrack with a line of pyramids running along the middle. Crowds cheered and called from the stands.

"It feels so real . . ." Niall gazed around. "How can such a big space fit into the operations room? It's like we've been dropped into the middle of a real-life chariot race!"

"The K-Casket plays tricks on your senses," Sam told him. "But something is very wrong. The game should be controlled by us, the players – not by the ghost of its old owner!"

"Mummy! Boy! Hurry up," King Tut snapped. "Choose a chariot and I'll give you the instructions."

A little uneasy now, Niall followed Sam towards a small, wooden, two-wheeled vehicle pulled by a pair of horses. Then he jumped as a blast of energy sparked in his head, and images shot through his mind. Suddenly he understood how best to drive the horses pulling the chariot.

"Of course, *I* did not need instructions." Sam had clearly felt a similar blast, and fanned his bandaged face with his hat. "In all my life I have only lost one chariot race."

"Wow!" Niall raised his eyebrows. "How many have you won?"

"Er, none! That time I lost was the only time I ever raced!"

"Great." Niall jumped into the chariot. "Still, who cares? It's only a game . . ."

He and Sam took hold of the reins, then Sam shouted at the horses – which jumped into life just as if they were real, and pulled the carriage to the starting line.

"Ready for your qualifying lap?" King Tut demanded.

Niall glanced at the five other chariot racers

lined up alongside. He gulped. "Er, yeah. Bring it!"

A voice from nowhere boomed out a count-down: "*Three, two, one, GOOOOOOO!*"

"YAHHH!" yelled Sam. He and Niall shook on the horses' reins, and the animals reared up and galloped away in a storm of dust. The crowd roared their approval as the chariots went thundering around the arena.

Niall's heart pounded as hooves kicked sand up into the air. The chariot rocked and rattled and banged as they neared the first turn, gaining speed. It felt so real!

 39

"Hold on, my friend!" Sam cried.

Niall leaned into the corner, gripping the reins tighter. Suddenly the chariot beside them hit a bump and its driver was thrown out. "AAARRRRRRRGH!" he yelled, tumbling away through the sand like a human wheel. His

horses charged on, out of control, still pulling the empty chariot behind them. It smashed against Sam and Niall's, and Niall nearly fell off.

"That was close!" he yelled. "Can't you use your powers, Sam?"

"Not in this game world, my friend. Hold on!" Holding the reins in his bandaged teeth, Sam kicked out at the empty chariot and managed to overturn it.

"Nice one!" Niall shook the reins of his sweating stallions, and their chariot edged ahead. The ground flew past beneath them. Niall gritted his teeth, and Sam held his hat to

 41

his head. Both yelled encouragement to their horses . . .

"We're winning!" Niall laughed. "Sam, we—"

"We have WON!" Sam jumped up in the air and shook his butt at the trailing chariots. "Oh, yes! Kiss my mummified bottom cheeks, all you who have *not* won!"

Niall high-fived him, and then together they reined the horses in to a trot.

A voice boomed out across the arena: "NEW HIGH SCORE SET! FASTEST QUALIFY-ING LAP *EVER*!"

"Wow! Check us!" Niall looked around and waved to the cheering crowds.

But Sam quickly pulled him back down. King Tut was running towards them.

"How dare you! You beat my *own* personal best time!"  He was hopping mad – hopping, jumping and fist-waving mad. "How *dare* you!"

"Er, sorry." Niall shrugged. "It's not like we were *trying* to beat you—"

43

"WHAT? You say you can beat me without even trying, eh?" King Tut's face screwed up with rage. "*Well?*"

"Er, no, sir!" Sam said quickly.

"You cheated!" Tut's dark eyes widened. "Admit it, you're cheats!"

Niall scowled. "We didn't cheat! How could we?"

"I am the greatest chariot racer ever. No one has ever beaten the great Tutankhamun!" He clapped his hands. "Beasts – to my side!"

In the blink of an eye, two huge dark animals appeared behind him. At the sight of Sam and

44

Niall, their red eyes narrowed, and drool splashed from their chops.

"I recognize those sphinxes," Niall breathed.

"I faced them in the *Train Those Sphinxes* simulation," Sam agreed. "King Tut has brought them here from an entirely different game world. But how?"

Niall gulped. "But they can't really hurt us, right? Like they didn't hurt you before. This is a game – it's not real— OW!"

45

The biggest sphinx had stepped forward and swiped the air. Sam and Niall jumped backwards, but the tip of a claw had caught Niall's arm. He gasped as he saw a bloody scratch there.

"Real enough for you?" Tut smiled as the sphinxes bared their savage teeth and pawed the sand, itching to be let loose. "Get these rotten cheaters, sphinxes! GET THEM!"

Chapter Four

Ghost in the Machine

Niall stared in horror at the advancing beasts. "Sam, this is going to be Game Over big-time – unless we can get back to reality!"

"Copy me, my young friend." Sam pressed two of the red stones on his KaBangle. "This will take us out of the game."

Niall pressed the same gems on his own KaBangle, and waited for the noisy arena to

vanish. Nothing happened. "We're stuck," he realized. "What's gone wrong?"

"Ha!" Tut laughed nastily. "My place, my rules. *I* decide if and when you may leave! And right now, my sphinxes want exercise . . . so you'd better RUN!"

The sphinxes roared so hard they blew Sam's hat off. "The boy gives good advice!"

"I'm running!" Niall was already pelting away. "Trust me, I'm running!"

The sphinxes charged after them. The other chariots scattered. The crowd roared loudly: "GET THEM! GET THEM!"

Niall dived and rolled as a huge sphinx claw almost sliced him in three. "Sam, what are we going to do?"

"Keep running!"

"Don't think so," said Tut. "Let's make things a bit more interesting . . ."

Niall gulped as he saw that the great stone walls of the arena were slowly closing in. "The space is getting smaller!"

The sphinxes stalked their prey in ever-tighter circles.

Sam leaped over a thick, swiping tail. "It is the very long shot, but let me try to use the ruby of transportation!" He pulled the bandages off his ribs, but before he could press the gadget, a

sphinx pounced and brought him to the ground. It snarled and opened its jaws . . .

"No!" Niall turned desperately to the watching King Tut. "Killing us won't change the fact that we beat your high score!" he said

quickly. "But that was just a qualifying lap, remember? Wouldn't it be better to beat us in a *proper* chariot race? Then you'll KNOW you're better than us. You can have us eaten without a care in the world!"

"Hmm." Tut held up a hand, and the crowd and the sphinxes stopped moving. The whole place had fallen silent, as if the game had been put on pause. "It's true that thrashing you totally would cheer me up," he said slowly. "Very well! We shall race!"

Phew, thought Niall. "Er, but first we need a break."

"I think I have been given many breaks already," called Sam weakly from beneath a whopping great paw. "My ribs have a break, my arms have a break, my left knee—"

"We shall race *now*, I say. NOW!" King Tut held up his right hand, and the arena began to crackle and glitch. "Wait . . . What is happening?"

Niall stared about in alarm as the sphinxes suddenly whirled away like paint down a plughole. The rest

of the arena was going the same way, and Tut too was breaking up and fading into darkness. "No!" the boy king cried. "You'll regret this! I WILL RETURRRRRRN . . . !"

With a dizzying jolt, Niall found himself back in the operations room, with Sam groaning on the floor beside him. "What happened?"

"Really, Mummy, why do you play silly games with the boy when you should be worshipping me?!" Great Mew waved a scrawny fist at Sam from the top of the fridge. "Well, I turned off your precious K-Casket,

53

so *there*. That'll teach you."

"Thank you, wondrous Mew!" Sam shook his limbs, which made several horrible cracking sounds. "Thank you from the bandaged backside of my heart!"

"Yeah, nice one, cat," Niall said shakily. He took off the KaBangle and dropped it on the floor. "Thanks."

"Why are you thanking me?" Mew frowned. "I'm not going to switch the silly thing back on again, you know."

But suddenly, with a soft whir and a sound like a gong, the K-Casket powered up again all

54

by itself. In the centre, a green light shone.

"OK," said Niall slowly, staring at the silvery casket. "That is totally creepy."

Sam unplugged the K-Casket, but the green "on" light refused to go out. "This also is creepy," he said. "The ghost of King Tut has great powers."

"King Tut?" said Mew. "Ghost? Eh? King Tut? Ehh? What? Ghost? Tut? ANSWER ME!!!"

Sam and Niall quickly told her what had happened.

"So you see, Great Mew, you saved our

lives!" Sam concluded.

"Lucky for your fish supplies," Niall added.

Mew yawned and jumped down from the fridge. "Well, I suggest that we dump that K-Casket back in the garage and forget all about it."

"What about Tut?" said Sam. "He is still inside the machine."

"So? He is not real," said Mew. "Simply an avatar."

Niall shivered. "A not-very-happy avatar that can think for itself."

"He thinks and acts like the real Tut," Sam

agreed, "but has no one to advise him – or to stop him when he goes too far."

"Pah!" Mew kicked the K-Casket. "I have no wish to be haunted by a digital ghost. Take that thing away!"

"Very well," Sam agreed. "How shall I repay your great kindness in saving our lives?"

"Spend less time tinkering with your so-called 'secret project' in the garage, for a start," said Mew grumpily. "Let Mumbum fix the old

wreck while you cook me some delicious fish suppers . . ."

Niall rolled his eyes. "If I can't help with this secret project, I guess I'll go home. After all that weirdness I could use a normality-check!"

"Of course." Sam gave him a big, bandaged thumbs-up. "Well, my friend, thank you for coming! Sorry my newly rediscovered games machine tried to kill us both! Next time, let us just have a cup of S."

"You mean *tea*," said Niall. "Bye!"

As Niall went back to his house, he was still shivering at the closeness of his escape from

the K-Casket. Tut's voice remained loud in his head: *I WILL RETURRRRRRN* . . .

The Snitch was sitting on the sofa, still playing her *Princess Pony Baloney* game, but for once Niall didn't mind. It looked bright and colourful. Safe.

"Er, Snitch," he said. "Mind if we go two-player?"

She stared at him like he'd grown seven heads. "*You* . . . want to play *Princess Pony Parlour* . . . with *me*?"

"Shut up." Niall grabbed the other controller. "Just tell me, which do we bring back to the

 59

stables first – the orange unicorn or the purple pony?"

Niall played for a good hour, but couldn't get rid of his uneasy feeling. He kept catching movement out of the corner of his eye, as if he was being watched. Finally, tired and spooked, he decided to have an early night.

"It's crazy to feel afraid in my own house," he told himself, lying in bed. "That digital Tut is trapped inside the K-Casket! He can't haunt anyone from there . . ."

But even as he spoke, a spooky golden glow appeared in the corner of his room. With a gasp

of horror, Niall pulled up his the duvet, peeping out from behind it. *This can't be happening!*

The ghostly face of King Tut was forming before him.

"Come back, boy," Tut said crossly. "Face me . . . *RACE* me . . . or I shall haunt you for ever more!"

Chapter Five

Watch Out – There's a Ghost About!

Niall opened his mouth, ready to shout for his mum . . . But what he got was a Mum*bum* – straight through the window!

SMAAAAASH!

Still wearing his Mechanic-Mutt suit, Mumbum flew

towards the floating face of Tutankhamun. He
went right through it, crashed into the wall and
then bounced back into Niall's lap. The robo-
dog barked crossly at the ghost of Tut, but the
boy king only smiled.

"Niall?" came Mum's sleepy voice from
across the landing. "What's all the noise?"

"Er, nothing!" Niall called quickly.

"Nothing, eh?" Tut looked even crosser as
his face grew larger, almost covering the wall.
"Is that what you think I am?"

A small strip of papyrus chuntered out of
Mumbum's mouth. On it was written:

GETT ON, NILE!
HOWLD ON TITE.

Niall quickly straddled the robo-dog's back and grabbed hold of his extra-pointy ears. Then, with a blast of his paw-jets that almost set fire to Niall's bed, Mumbum whooshed away through the broken window. Niall clung on tight as they flew through the cold night air towards the Pyra-Base, and prayed his pyjama bottoms would stay on.

Sam was waiting in the hallway, in a bandaged nightgown and nightcap, looking worried.

"Thanks for coming to get me, boy." Niall patted Mumbum's bandaged butt. "Now, if you could also tell my mum who broke my window and burned the duvet, that would be perfect."

"I shall fix this for you with a Spell of Putting Right," Sam declared. He stepped outside and pointed at Niall's bedroom. Another window shattered. "Ooops. I shall fix that with magic too." He pointed again. The faint sound of an explosion carried through the night. "Er . . ."

"That's probably enough fixing for now," said Niall hurriedly. "Listen, Sam, I saw King Tut's face in my room!"

"I feared that this might happen," Sam said gravely. "That is why I sent Mumbum to guard you."

"But how did you know?"

"Because . . . I *too* have seen his image. Here in the base." Sam looked uneasy. "The K-Casket is turned off and unplugged . . . and yet still he appears in our world."

"Maybe he's just using up the last bit of power stored there," Niall said hopefully. "He'll run out soon, and stay out of our hair."

"Tutankhamun is in my hair?" Sam yanked off his nightcap and felt all around his bandaged

67

head. "Wait. I do not *have* hair! You must be mistaken, Niall."

"YOU DON'T GET RID OF ME THAT EASILY . . ." With a golden glow, King Tut's face appeared above them.

"*EEEEK!*" Niall and Sam clung together in fright.

Tut's image burst into ghostly laughter. "Be seeing you . . . soon."

The glow faded and the face disappeared.

Niall cleared his throat and let go of Sam. "Let's hope King Tut gets bored quickly and gives up."

Sam twisted his hands into strange shapes. "I am keeping all my fingers circled."

"Try crossing them," Niall said glumly. "I only wish we'd never crossed Tut!"

"We must rest and get strength," said Sam. "Return to your bed, my friend. Mumbum will guard you as you sleep."

So Niall hitched a ride with Mumbum back to his bedroom. The metal dog hovered outside while Sam fixed the damage to the windows. (After accidentally setting fire to the carpet. Twice.)

★ ★ ★

69

Niall finally fell asleep around 3 a.m. He didn't stir until Mum woke him for school. With a quiet "Woof", the faithful Mumbum returned to the Pyra-Base.

"Perhaps the ghost has gone," Niall said hopefully.

But as he cleaned his teeth that morning, he saw King Tut's face looking back at him from the mirror.

"Race me!" said the ghostly boy.

"*ARGGHHHHH!*"

Niall threw his toothbrush

into the air and ran out of the bathroom in his pyjamas, white foam dripping from his open mouth.

The Snitch, waiting outside, shrieked. "Mum! I think Niall's got rabies!"

"Look in the bathroom!" Niall stared at her, wide-eyed. "Go on, look!"

She strolled in. "What am I looking at? You've left a mess in the basin, but what else is new?"

"You can't see anything?"

Ellie yawned. "Stop being dumb."

Niall wiped his mouth on his sleeve and shuddered.

Worse was to come. At school, in Maths, the ghost of King Tut appeared AGAIN – just behind Mrs Crabtree, Niall's grumpy old teacher.

"Race me!" the ghost demanded once more.

Niall gave a start and stifled a cry.

"Stop mucking around, Rivers!" Mrs Crabtree roared. "Detention after school!"

Niall spent the rest of the day feeling edgy and miserable. No one else had caught sight of the ghost. Like

the Pyra-Base, King Tut's spooky image seemed to be something that only Niall, with his powers from the KaBa relic, could see.

Detention time came round. Niall was sitting alone in his form room working through a maths sheet when he saw King Tut's face.

"RACE ME!" Tut shouted. "Oh, c'mon. You and the mummy are no fun at all!"

"Can't you take a hint?" said Niall through gritted teeth. "We don't want to race!"

"You know you do really. It's just one race."

"NO WAY!" Niall shouted.

Mrs Crabtree stuck her head through the

 73

door. "Shouting in the classroom?" she boomed. "Another detention!"

Niall groaned, and put his head on his desk. "Looks like this ghost's not going anywhere in a hurry . . . while *I'm* going round the bend!"

Once detention was over, Niall ran home and went straight next door to the Pyra-Base. "Sam!" he called. "We've got to do something about Tut! He turned up at school and got me into trouble. Has he shown up here too?"

"Three times!" Sam came out of the operations room wearing greasy blue overalls over his bandages. "It has been most disruptive

to my secret project. Every time Tut turns up I jump with surprise and bang my head on it." Lifting his hat, he revealed three egg-shaped bumps. "Behold!"

"At least your lumps come with ready-made bandages," Niall pointed out. "Hey, what *is* this special project of yours? You haven't told me."

"WHO CARES?" came the familiar voice of Tut behind them.

Niall and Sam jumped in the air.

"Now, then. Who's for a rrrrrrrrace?" Tut looked from one to the other. "A gentle, non-competitive, definitely not-resulting-in-your-terrible-death chariot race?"

Sam looked at Niall and lowered his voice. "Perhaps we should race and let him win so he will go away?"

"Have you forgotten what happened last time?" Niall hissed back. "We'll be totally in his power! He might decide he wants to *keep* beating us – over and over again."

"And never let us go," Sam said with a shiver.

76

"Until I starve to death," Niall added, "or we crash and die, or get eaten by sphinxes—"

"You have convinced me, my friend." Sam stuck out his tongue at Tut. "We will not race. Nyah nyah nyah!"

Tut scowled. "I'll never leave you alone until you agree to race me! NEVER!"

As the ghost vanished in sparkling light, Niall turned to Sam. "What can we do to shut him up?"

Sam sighed. "I think the time has come to read the K-Casket's instruction manual."

"The manual? Wow, things *are* serious!"

Niall pulled a face. "Does it come with a chapter on 'What to do if your K-Casket is haunted by the digital ghost of a long-dead pharaoh?'"

"Perhaps!" said Sam seriously. "There must be some way to drain the console of all power . . ."

"So get on with it!" Mew poked her head out of the operations room. "You can be rid of your phantom pharaoh, and concentrate on me again!" She smiled primly. "The instruction manual will be in the file store, Mummy. I'm sure the boy will help – won't you, boy? Oh, and

chop-chop, if you please! Then you can cook me some kippers. MEEOOOOOOOOOW!"

Mew sauntered away, and Niall glowered after her. "I'd like to stick those kippers where the sun god doesn't shine!" Then he turned to Sam. "Still, she's right. The sooner we drain that K-Casket the better."

"Yes! Bravo. Blessed are those who drain the power from K-Caskets. Woo-hoo! Yay! Only . . ." Sam's bandaged face had fallen. "Only, I was so happy when I found the K-Casket again. I wished to use it, because . . . it is the closest I will ever come to going back

to KaBa — the home that I shall never see again."

"Of course . . ." Niall remembered how happy Sam had seemed. "I'm sorry the ghost of King Tut has spoiled it."

"Cursed be his over-competitive spirit!" Sam blew his nose on a bandaged handkerchief. "Come, my friend. To the stores. Let us begin!"

Chapter Six

A Lesson in Store

Sam led the way along the sandstone corridor, through the Pyra-Base kitchen, the ostrich egg hatchery and the laundry room (which had an actual stream running through it) – then turned left into a part of the Pyra-Base Niall had never seen before. It was dustier and dimmer, lit by flickering torches mounted on the walls.

"We do not use the old file store much," Sam confessed, opening a heavy stone door. "Lionel needs his rest."

"Lionel? Who's Lionel?" Niall almost choked on the musty pong that wafted out. The file store seemed vast; he saw long rows of triangular bookcases vanishing into shadows. The floor was covered in reeds and stagnant pools. An old ibis, its body bandaged, with crooked black legs and a long, curved beak, struggled to rise from a scruffy nest beside the door.

"Greetings, Librarian Lionel." Sam bowed to

the bird. "May I have the K-Casket instruction manual, if you would be so kind?"

Librarian Lionel bowed stiffly in return, and gave a loud squawk. Then he flapped uncertainly away – and banged into a bookcase. Niall frowned as the bird fell to the floor in a flurry of fallen scrolls. Lionel pecked at a couple, as if trying to pick them up, then, with another squawk, splashed away on foot.

"Wow. He looks really on the ball," Niall remarked.

"Hush, Niall! No balls are allowed in the file store! A carelessly thrown ball could knock scrolls off a shelf! And then how would Lionel find anything?"

"He's a bird! How can a bird find anything anyway?"

"The ibis is wise. Do you not recall that great Thoth, god of writing and knowledge, had the head of an ibis?"

There was a loud crash as the bird bumped into another bookcase and knocked it over. Niall

winced. "Lionel must have got through a few heads in his time! Did you train him yourself?"

"Yes! How did you know?"

"Just a lucky guess."

After what felt like an age, Lionel came back, dragging a sack of scrolls across the soggy floor. Sam bowed again as he took the scrolls. Lionel bowed in return, squawked, and went to sit on his nest again, looking dizzy.

Niall felt the same after rummaging inside

the sack. There had to be seventy scrolls in there!
"Your people didn't believe in a quick-start guide,
huh?" He upended the sack and spotted a black
scroll with red symbols on the side. "Here you go
– *What to Do if Things Go Wrong*."

With a sad smile, Sam reached out to take it.

"Think you can get rid of me, do you?" In
a flash, King Tut's ghostly head
appeared right above them.
"Well, you can't! You'll never
take away my power."

"Leave us alone!" Niall
shouted.

"You cannot give orders to a king!" said the ghostly golden face. "No one has ever beaten me. No one has ever disobeyed me and not been punished!"

"Why can you not play nicely?" Sam demanded. "We could get along and be happy."

"Because I'm the ruler of all Egypt!" Tut retorted. "And you are lowly, rotten cheats. Nothing you do can stop me haunting you!"

The golden face shimmered and faded away.

"What a creep." Niall shuddered. "They should've named him Tutankha-*loon*. Can't we just smash the K-Casket?"

"No, no, indeed. If the power inside were to escape, it could be most dangerous." Sam took the scroll and unrolled it. "But to drain the K-Casket of its power safely will take time. I will need an energy-leech and many connecting cables. Mumbum must leave my secret project and help me in the workshop instead."

"Whatever your secret project is . . ." said Niall pointedly, but Sam only tapped his bandaged nose. "I'm sorry *I* can't stay and help, but Mum will be expecting me home. I'd better split." He paused. "Why don't I double-check the rest of the scrolls? Perhaps there's something

else we can try if the power-draining doesn't work."

"I doubt it, my friend," said Sam sadly. "But I thank you in any bag."

"You mean, *case*," Niall told him with a smile. "See you soon."

Niall took the sack of scrolls home with him, hiding it behind his back as he sneaked in through the kitchen. By the time Mum had given him a telling-off for being so late, he'd stashed it in the cupboard under the stairs.

He ate tea in a daydream, too distracted even to tease the Snitch properly. At any moment,

he half expected the ghost of King Tut to start haunting him again.

"Think I'll get an early night, Mum," said Niall. "Night!" Ignoring her shocked look, he sneaked his secret sack of scrolls upstairs with him.

By the light of his desk lamp, Niall pored over each ancient papyrus, making sense of the mysterious squiggles. As the hours passed and he worked his way through the tongue-twisting hieroglyphs, his eyes began to ache.

It was nearly 11.30 when he reached a scroll that listed the activities on the K-Casket's KaBa menu. There was a real mix – everything from *Tour the City of the Dead* to *Stewing Swans for Pleasure and Profit.*

Niall's eyes strayed to a small section at the bottom of the scroll marked *Advanced Lessons.* One of them explained, *Reverse your K-Casket's power settings in case of accidental draining.*

"Wait a minute . . ." Niall thought aloud. "Tut's digital ghost has been stuck in the K-Casket for so long, he could have done every lesson a hundred times." He remembered Tut's taunting

words: *Nothing you do can stop me haunting you!*

"So, if Sam starts trying to drain the power with his energy-leech, Tut can reverse the settings in the K-Casket – and *absorb* power instead."

Niall switched off his light and looked out of the window: the lights of the Pyra-Base were flickering on and off, glowing with unearthly energy.

Sam must be trying to drain Tut's power right now, Niall realized. *He could be playing right into the ghost's hands. I've got to stop him, before it's too late!*

Chapter Seven

The Ghost with the Most!

Niall swung his legs over the sill and reached
for the drainpipe that ran
down beside his window.
The plastic creaked alarm-
ingly under his weight, but
he dropped down onto
the box hedge outside the
lounge and, from there,
raced to the bottom of the

garden where he could cross the fence.

A hum of power filled the air as Niall approached the Pyra-Base. The door seemed to be locked. "Sam, wait!" he shouted. "You've got to stop! Instead of draining Tut's energy, I think you're *feeding* it!"

Again and again he hammered on the door, until Mew finally opened it. "Meeowwww *dare* you disturb me at this late hour!"

"We've got to stop Sam messing with that K-Casket," Niall panted.

"Because he should be concentrating on serving me?" Mew nodded thoughtfully. "You

are right to be concerned, of course, but on this occasion—"

"Come on!" Niall pushed past the snooty cat goddess. The whole corridor was trembling with power.

Finally he reached the workshop. "Sam, wait!" Niall threw open the door, and was dazzled by an incredible lightshow. The energy-leech looked like a large stone jar with buttons and an aerial. Orbs of light crackled from it and spun around the glowing, pulsing K-Casket. "Sam?"

"Stay back, my friend!" Sam shouted.

95

Mumbum flew down from a corner of the workshop and barked a warning at Niall. "The energy-leech has gone wrong."

"It must be Tut!" Niall yelled back. "Sam, you've got to unplug that thing."

"I have tried." Sam held up blackened fingers. "I cannot! The K-Casket is drawing power not only from the energy-leech but from the Base itself!"

Niall stared in horror. "How much energy is that?"

"Too much!" Sam cried.

Then, with an ear-splitting, shuddering

BOOM, the energy-leech exploded like a firework. The power was sucked into the K-Casket, which rattled and steamed in the sudden silence. The workshop was now dark, lit only by the emergency lighting – flickering torches attached to the wall.

Sam stared at the K-Casket. "All the power of the Pyra-Base has been sucked inside there!"

"I've got a bad feeling about this," said Niall.

Suddenly the K-Casket started to shake like

a china plate in an earthquake. Niall and Sam looked at each other as a rattling, juddering sound started up from inside the console, getting louder all the time . . .

The K-Casket shone blinding white – and two wild, snorting dark stallions came galloping out of it, pulling a splendid golden chariot. Niall and Sam dived aside, and Mumbum whooshed up into the air; all three barely escaped the thundering procession in time.

"Freeeeeeeee!" came a familiar boyish cry. "Free at last!"

98

Sam looked round and gasped. "Oh, no . . ."

"Oh, YES!" King Tut laughed as he steered his chariot around the workshop. "After thousands of years, I have form! I have substance! I have weight!"

Tutankhamun no longer looked ghostly. His avatar had been made flesh! It was as if the real boy king was there in the workshop, with real horses pulling a real chariot!

"Thanks to the energy you so kindly allowed me to absorb, I have escaped my digital prison." Tut leaned out and tipped over a workbench. "Ha! I can touch real things. *Really* real things!

At last I am free of the K-Casket and LOOSE in the real world!"

"And we're in real trouble," Niall groaned.

"Kindly stop knocking things over!" Sam cried. "The workshop is not a place for chariot races!"

Tut pulled on the reins, staring angrily at Sam. "How dare you seek to command me, Mummy! You were put here to serve the pharaoh – and I demand that you race me at once." He pointed to the K-Casket, and in another flash of light two more horses emerged. They looked tired and skinny as they pulled

101

an old rickety chariot on wonky wheels.

"You want us to race in that?" Niall grimaced. "How is that fair?"

"If you have anything better to race in, feel free to use it!" Now Tut leaned over and picked

up the K–Casket, placing it carefully beside him in his chariot. "Come on, both of you. Start racing. Do as I say."

"I will NOT serve you," Sam said stoutly, "because you are NOT the real Tut."

"Did the king not make me in his image?" Tut protested. "Did he not create me with his mind? And am I not now just as real as he was?"

"Whatever you look like, you're just a program created to learn lessons and play games!" Niall told him. "The real Tut wouldn't go crazy like this."

103

"*I* will be the boy he never got the chance to be in life," Tut countered. "Cheeky, strong and completely in charge!"

"Not true. You are an intruder in *my* Pyra-Base." Sam whistled to Mumbum. "Come, my fine dog – intruders must be caught and dealt with!"

"*Arf!*" woofed Mumbum. He zoomed down like a mutt-shaped missile to tackle Tut. But Tut ducked, grabbed a bronze-tipped spear from the floor of his chariot and hurled it at the robo-dog. With incredible accuracy, the spear pierced a paw-jet, causing smoke and sparks

to shoot out. With a yap of surprise, Mumbum spiralled down and struck the floor with a bang that made the skinny horses rear up in alarm.

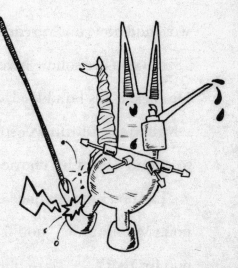

"Mumbum!" yelled Sam and Niall together.

"Ha!" Tut patted the K-Casket. "The javelin training game has come in very handy!"

Mumbum shook his bandaged tail to show Sam and Niall that he was all right. But Sam

 105

was mad now, and already racing to the attack. "Since you are solid – here's sand in your eyes!" He flicked his bandaged wrist, and suddenly a whirling sandstorm was spinning past the horses to engulf Tut in his chariot.

The boy king coughed and spluttered. "Curse you, Mummy . . . you'll pay for that!"

Niall gasped as he saw another bronze-tipped spear hurtle out of the sandstorm – heading straight for Sam!

Chapter Eight

A World of His Own

Niall knew there was no way Sam could dodge the spear in time.

Luckily, he didn't have to.

Like a shot, the mummy pulled hard on a bandage dangling from his wrist and yelled, "*Shield Surprise!*"

A triangular leather shield burst through his bandages, protecting him from neck to waist! The spear bounced off harmlessly.

 107

"Wow!" Niall marvelled. "That really *was* a surprise!"

But as the spear fell, the wooden end hit the leg of one of Tut's horses. It reared up with a loud neigh – and so did its neighbour. Next moment Sam had to leap aside again as the two horses bolted for the workshop doors . . . and went crashing straight through them, dragging Tut and the K-Casket along behind.

108

"I'll blow away your sandstorm, Mummy!" the phantom pharaoh shouted. "It is time I tasted fresh air once more . . ."

"He's heading for the outside world," Niall realized. "Should we go after him?"

"I fear we must." Sam was checking Mumbum; the dog's metal nose was wonky and his tail wagged weakly. "But poor Mumbum cannot transport us."

"We'll have to follow on foot," said Niall.

"Not so, my friend." Sam pointed to the scrawny horses and lopsided chariot Tut had summoned for them. "Behold – transport!"

Niall sighed and jumped in. "I reckon we'd be quicker on foot!"

Sam absorbed his Shield Surprise back into his bandages and got in beside Niall. "Come, horses, if you please." He shook the reins. "Giddy-down!" The horses trotted off, wheezing as they went. "Follow that king!"

But Tutankhamun was already some way ahead. The sandstorm had cleared, and his chariot sped along the great wide corridors. As he burst into the hallway, Great Mew was leaving the operations room with a mouthful of minnow. She spat it out with a wail of fright and leaped high into the air – so high that she actually somersaulted over Tut's head as he thundered by.

"HELLLPPPPPPP!" Mew wailed, clinging to the ceiling by her claws. "Police!

111

Murder! Haddock! MEEOOOWWWW!"

Sam and Niall appeared soon after, hot on Tut's trail. As they passed underneath, Mew dropped down into Sam's lap.

"What do you think you're doing," she cried, "allowing that shoddy replica Tut to almost squish me like a flatfish?"

"We didn't let him loose," Niall spluttered as their puffing horses towed them out into the garden. "Tut's K-Casket avatar absorbed a ton of energy and made himself real!"

"What?" Mew looked outraged. "The cheek of pharaohs' digital ghosts today!"

"The last 'today' he knew was three thousand years ago," Sam reminded her. "I fear he will find Niall's world a very strange place indeed . . ."

From a nearby street came the sound of honking horns, screeching brakes and screams. "Uh-oh," said Niall. "It sounds like the world finds Tut a very strange *pharaoh* indeed!"

"Freed from the K-Casket, he has become visible to all," Mew agreed.

"We must learn what is happening!" Sam urged the horses faster. Niall held on tight as their chariot rattled on – through a big hole in the neighbour's fence, over the garden

 113

beyond, down a side-alley, and out onto the main road.

Then his jaw dropped so far it nearly bruised his toes.

King Tut was riding his chariot down the middle of the high street! Cars on either side were swerving out of the way, mounting the pavement, crashing into lampposts. A lorry honked its horn as it was forced off the road, and knocked over a postbox. People were shouting and police sirens sounded in the distance. Tut's horses stopped and reared up in fear at the noisy clamour around them.

"What world of madness is this?" The boy king stared around. "This noisy, smelly world of hard ground, and metal chariots with no beasts to pull them, and buildings like big brick boxes?"

"This is one of the nicer neighbourhoods!" Sam jumped down from the rickety chariot. "Why not return to the world you know, inside the K–Casket?"

"Surrender my solid form? Go back to sleep, half alive inside a machine?" Tut sneered and shook his head. "No. King Tut was born to rule, and that is my destiny too. But first I think

116

I'll bring a few familiar things from my digital home . . ."

"Uh-oh," said Niall. "What does he mean?"

Tut had raised his arms towards the heavens, ignoring angry shouts and raised fists from people all around him. Rings of golden energy were forming around his hands. The K-Casket trembled at his side as he raised his voice and called:

"O Casket of Power,

By magic transmit

The beasts of KaBa

That dwell in the pit!"

The ground shook, and white flashes like lightning filled the air. "What's happening?" Niall shouted.

"He is taking something else out of the K-Casket." Mew's fur stood on end. "*Sphinxes!*"

There was a terrifying roar, and Niall's heart sank. He turned to find that one of the massive monsters had appeared in the middle

of the street. Muscles rippled
over the lion's body, and
the round, noseless face
showed confusion and
anger.

Tut nodded in satisfaction.
"My little pet here will guard
you – while *I* plan out the route
for our chariot race!"

The sphinx watched its master ride off along
the bus lane, overtaking a taxi on the way.
Its big eyes narrowed as it took in Sam, Niall
and Mew.

 119

But then its attention turned to the crowds of frightened people all around . . .

"Just what the town centre needed," said Niall. "Savage killer monsters!"

"At least things cannot get any worse!" said Sam.

But they could, of course.

The sphinx growled at the nearest terrified onlookers. Jaws open wide, it leaped towards them.

Chapter Nine

Jaws of the Sphinx

"Bad boy!" Sam cried. "No eating humans!" As the huge beast jumped through the air, he flicked out his wrist to launch a bandage lasso. He looped it around the beast's neck and tugged with all his mummy muscle-power, pulling it to the ground. With his other hand he lassoed the fallen postbox, and with a grunt of effort jerked it through the air. It smashed into the

sphinx's open jaws!

"MRRRRPPPHHHHH!"

Tangled in bandages, the sphinx snarled, but the postbox was wedged tight. "There!" Sam cried. "An instant gobstruction."

"*Ob*struction—" Niall began. Then he grinned. "No, on second thoughts, you were right first time. That's a good word for something caught in your mouth!"

All around, terrified people were running for cover. "Stay out of sight!" Sam yelled.

"Lock the doors!"

"Throw out any fish you might have!" Mew added.

"Ignore that," Niall told them, with a sideways glance at the snooty cat. "Is food all you can think about?"

"No. I can also think about running away!" Great Mew had adjusted her tiara and was waiting in the chariot. "Come on. While Tut's off planning his route . . ."

Niall wasn't convinced. "There's no getting out of this race. He'll come after us wherever we go."

123

"Our only chance of getting rid of Tut is to win the race," said Sam. "And there is only one way to do that."

"Oh, yes?" Mew waved at the weedy horses. "What will you do – inflate these noble steeds with a bicycle pump?"

"I agree with your first plan, Great Mew," said Sam. "Come! To the Pyra-Base we must fly!"

Leaving the giant beast to swat at its bright red gobstruction, Sam and Niall jumped in the chariot beside Mew. Sam shook the reins, and the scrawny horses trotted back the way they'd

come. "I hope we have time," the mummy said. "If my plan fails, we sit no chance!"

"*Stand*," Niall told him.

"I am already standing, my friend!"

Stomach churning, Niall held on tight as Sam drove through the trashed gardens and broken fences left in Tut's wake. As they neared the Pyra-Base, Sam urged the horses on.

Suddenly a sphinx jumped out at them from behind a fence!

"Arghhh!" Niall shouted. "How many of those things did Tut summon from the K-Casket?"

125

Sam frowned. "I fear the answer is MANY."

The horses reared up, but the sphinx swatted them to the ground and opened its horrible mouth. *CHOMP!* As the beast chowed down, the horses vanished in a blast of pixels.

"I fear it will find *real* living things like us far tastier," Sam shouted. "Run!"

"Every cat for herself!" Mew meowed, shooting off towards the Pyra-Base.

"Wait!" Niall pointed over the fence at another sphinx standing in his back garden. "Mum and the Snitch are in the house!"

"Perhaps they have not noticed anything amiss?" Sam said brightly.

A piercing shriek burst from the Snitch's bedroom.

"I think maybe they have." Niall grabbed Sam's arm. "We've got to help them!"

"Of course, my friend." Without hesitation, Sam picked up Niall and threw him over the fence . . .

And *SPLAT!* into the compost heap.

Sam vaulted the fence and landed beside Niall with a *SPLOOSH!* He shook muck off his bandages and beamed. "There! A perfect soft landing!"

"I thought we were in deep doo-doo before – now I *know* it!" Niall jumped up as another ear-splitting Snitch-shriek echoed from his house. "Come on!"

They ran up the garden together – but as they

did so, two sphinxes came crashing through the patio doors, ears back, eyes narrowed, racing towards them.

Niall stared in horror. "They'll squash us flat!"

"*Pharaoh's Fire!*" cried Sam, and a ball of flame burst from his bandaged palm. He prepared to hurl it at the nearest sphinx . . .

But as the Snitch screamed again, the sphinxes quickened their pace and shot straight past Sam and Niall.

"What are they chasing?" Niall wondered.

"Nothing." Sam blew out his fiery hand,

and pointed. "I think *they* are the ones being chased!"

The Snitch had followed them out of the house, fists clenched, a fierce look on her face. "And don't you dare try scaring my mum again!" she bellowed.

Niall ran up to her.

"Snitch? What are you—?"

"Oh, typical," she groaned.

"Thanks, Niall. I'm having a lovely dream about scaring away monsters, and YOU have to show up in it."

"A dream?" Niall shook his head. "This isn't a dream, you muppet! Those sphinx things can totally get you."

"They can't," the Snitch said smugly. "They're scared of me. They don't like me screaming. I screamed so loudly, one of them wet himself!"

"That must be the widdle of the sphinx," said Sam solemnly.

Niall's mum came out to join them. "You know, it's quite a strange dream, this one," she said. "It must be that cheese I ate before bed."

"Er . . . yeah. A dream," said Niall awkwardly. "So don't worry about the mess in the

 131

garden, OK? It's not real." A thought occurred to him. "Hey, if the Snitch's screams really *do* scare sphinxes, how about looking for more to terrify – before they eat anyone they shouldn't?"

The Snitch gave a big smile. "I'm up for that!"

"Come on then, darling," said Mum, and together they ran off, waving to Sam as they went.

"Your small sister proves to be a big

beast-tamer!" Sam observed. "Blessed be her powerful lung capacity! My lungs were strong also – before they were taken out and put in a canopic jar."

Niall grimaced. "Nice story. You should write it on a scroll so Lionel can lose it someplace."

"There is no time for that now, my friend," said the mummy seriously. "We must hurry to the Pyra-Base and find Mumbum. For if this plan of mine fails, I fear it will be the end for us all!"

Chapter Ten

Dealing in Danger

In the Pyra-Base workshop, Mumbum was back on his paws with a frightened Lionel sitting on his back.

"Mumbum, my proud hound," said Sam, patting the bandaged bot. "And Lionel! Greetings."

The ibis nodded stiffly to a scroll and gave a solemn "CAW".

Niall picked it up and unrolled it. "What's this?"

Sam had a look. "Lionel has written his own scroll of knowledge!"

"*Now that he has absorbed the entire power supply of the Pyra-Base,*" Niall read aloud, "*King Tut's deranged digital avatar will have complete control over anything taken from the K-Casket's game world . . .*"

"This is not comforting," said Sam.

"Caw," said Lionel, a little defensively.

"Where's the cat?" wondered Niall.

"The cat *goddess* is sensibly in hiding," called Great Mew from inside a pyramid–shaped

toolbox. "And she'll stay there while you *take* a hiding!"

"Thanks a bunch," Niall muttered.

"We are not beaten yet," said Sam. "Mumbum! Will you kindly give my special secret project in the garage some final checks?"

The robo-dog woofed and spluttered out of the workshop on his battered jets.

"Sam, aren't you ever going to tell me what this secret project IS?" Niall complained.

A chill wind blew through the workshop, and a golden glow appeared above them. Lionel flapped wonkily over to the toolbox and hid behind it.

"I cannot tell you of my secret project now, my friend," Sam whispered, "for I fear King Tut has found we are gone and come looking . . ."

He was right. A great golden face appeared, peering down through a swirling, glittering dust-cloud high above. The angry face of King Tut.

"So! You ran away, did you?" he bellowed. "Because you know I can beat you any time!"

"Actually," said Sam, "we *rode* away in our chariot – until one of your sphinxes ate our horses."

"Then it looks as if I will win our race by default," gloated Tut. "Unless you can find something else to ride . . . ? A three-legged camel, perhaps? Ha ha ha!"

"We *do* have something else we can race in," Sam said.

"Fine! Bring it outside then, and let's get on

with it." Tut smirked. "But you won't win, you know."

Niall glared up at him. "Where is this race taking place? How will we know where to go?"

"You'll know because you'll be following the trail of my dust," Tut bragged. "In any case, I've decided your human roads are too clogged with strange chariots to be any good for racing. So I'm going to take a level out of the K–Casket's chariot game and place it out here in your world . . ."

"A level you've played about a million times

before, so you know every twist and turn," said Niall. "Is that fair?"

Tut smiled. "There is no way you can ever beat me again!"

"Then let us make the race more interesting, yes?" Sam smiled. "If you win the race, you can do what you like with us. But if *we* win . . . you must return to the virtual world in which you belong and stay there. Do you accept?"

"Ha! Fine!" Tut nodded. "You have my word as a king. Now come outside. Let the race commence!"

The golden face faded from view.

"He's super-confident," Niall sighed, turning to Sam. "Whatever this secret project of yours is, I hope it's speedy."

"Speedy? You have seen nothing not yet – none have, for it was hidden under a blanket!" Sam rubbed his bandaged hands, then clapped them together. "Mumbum? Bring in . . . the car-sophagus!"

"*Car-soff-a-guss*?" Niall struggled to say the word – then struggled to find words at all as a bizarre vehicle careered through the wrecked workshop doors.

It looked like a kind of oversized stone coffin

on six wheels; *pyramid*-shaped wheels, with triangular tyres. It was painted in blue and black and gold. A large engine made of gleaming precious metals was mounted on the back.

"I call it a car-sophagus because it looks like a sarcophagus but is really a car!" Sam beamed.

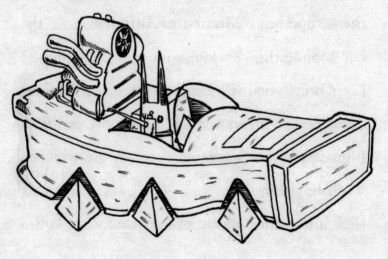

"A most funny joke, yes?"

Niall pulled a face. "I may die laughing."

"That would be fitting – since a sarcophagus is what Ancient Egyptians put their dead bodies in." Mew had popped her head out of the tool-box. "Vehicles like this were driven only by the richest and most powerful of our realm . . ."

"I found this car-sophagus in an abandoned Pyra-Base, one thousand years ago," Sam explained. "Finders keepers, yes? Now and then I have been tinkling in it."

"You mean, *tinkering with* it," said Niall. "At least, I hope you do! Is it fast?"

"My friend, it has a six-hundred camel-power engine!" Sam opened the driver's door, and Mumbum hopped out. "It will be much faster than Tut's chariot."

Niall considered. "It feels like we're cheating a bit. But then, Tut isn't exactly playing fair either, is he?"

"We shall win the race and all will be well!" Sam paused. "So long as the engine does not fall off and explode!"

Niall frowned. "Is that likely?"

"Well . . . in truth, the car-sophagus is not fully tested," Sam admitted. "I have not yet

finished working on it. But Mumbum will travel in the boot with all his tools, in case of trouble."

"The boot is in the back, right?"

"What strange ideas you have, Niall!" Sam pointed as a large stone boot rose up from under the bonnet.

"Riiiight," said Niall.

As Mumbum jumped inside the boot and hid from sight, Sam opened the passenger door for Niall. A triangular steering wheel dominated the dashboard, surrounded by buttons marked with different hieroglyphs. Niall got in and winced – the seat was solid stone. "You . . .

know how to drive this thing?"

"Of course!" Sam gripped what looked like a metal gearstick and it snapped off in his hand. "Well, mostly. I am sure this was not important." He threw the gearstick out of the window and took the wheel. "Now, my friend. Are you ready for the ride of your life?"

The car-sophagus' engine rumbled into growling, wailing life. Inside, the stone seats shook. Symbols lit up on the dashboard. Two fluffy pyramid-shaped dice swayed beneath the rearview mirror.

"Here goes everything," Niall murmured.

Sam floored the accelerator pedal, and the incredible car sped out of the workshop and along the wide corridors of the Pyra-Base . . . ready for the final showdown.

Chapter Eleven

A Dirty, Desperate Race

The car-sophagus roared out through the front door of the Pyra-Base. Niall gasped. The familiar overgrown garden, the fence, his own house next door – all these things had vanished! Around them they saw a very strange land indeed.

"I . . ." Sam's eyes were shiny with tears. "I do not believe it!"

There were pyramids everywhere. Yellow trees grew with pointy pyramids of leaves. The red hills were shaped like pyramids, dotted with bushes like upturned pyramids. Rows of proper stone pyramids, all different colours and sizes, stretched out on either side of a rubbery pink road.

"It is KaBa!" Sam said. "I am . . . home!"

"So this is how things are where you're from?" Niall gazed around at the weird,

colourful beauty. The sky above was dark green, and filled with moons and shooting stars. But it looked blurry, like a picture enlarged too far. It didn't feel quite real.

Because it's not real, Niall reminded himself. *It's just a videogame landscape that's been taken out of the console.*

Sam grinned. "Is KaBa not wonderful?"

"Not wonderful? Totally." Niall nodded. "Looks like Lionel was right – Tut the nut can turn *anything* from his digital world into reality. Even a huge chunk of the landscape!"

"Hmm?" Sam hardly seemed to hear him;

he was gazing about in pure delight. "Ah, yes. Truly his powers are great. Oh, Niall. To see KaBa makes me most very happy."

"I'll soon wipe the smile off your face!" cried Tutankhamun, appearing in his chariot from behind the nearest pyramid.

"Where's my house gone, and my mum and my sister?" Niall demanded. "Come to think of it, where's the whole *town* gone?"

"Safely inside the K-Casket!" Tut patted the console, which still sat by his feet. "The surrounding area has simply swapped places with my digital world."

"Are my mum and the Snitch OK in your box of tricks?"

"They are perfectly safe – provided nothing happens to the K-Casket . . ." The boy king scowled as he took in the extraordinary car-sophagus. "Wait. What trickery is this?"

Sam leaned out of the window. "You said you could beat us whatever we ride in."

"I totally can," Tut agreed. "You don't think I became the K-Casket's Top Record Racer without learning a few tricks, do you?"

With a flick of the reins, he made his horses turn their rear ends towards the car-sophagus:

they raised their tails in the air.

Niall covered his eyes. "I'm not sure I want to see this trick!"

When the horses' tails were fully raised, a jet of blue flame came out of their bottoms!

Sam gasped. "Horses with rocket bums?"

"So you were never going to play fair anyway," Niall shouted.

"I can do whatever I want to *anything* I want. And I want to beat you." The boy king smiled. "Ready to race?"

Sam put his bandaged foot on the accelerator. "Ready!"

"Then, three, two, one, GO!" Tut shook the reins, and the rocket-powered horses zoomed away.

"After him!" Niall yelled.

Sam stamped down on the pedal. Six pyramid-shaped wheels spun on the rubbery road, then the car-sophagus roared away, swift as a spaceship.

"WHOAAAAAAAAA!" Niall yelled. "I think you left my stomach behind!"

"I will try to pick it up on the second lap!" Sam promised.

The road through the strange KaBa land-scape was full of sharp turns; Niall was flung this way and that. He caught a blur of blue fields, shielded his eyes from the glare of golden rivers. Ahead, he saw the silhouette of Tut's chariot; smoke was trailing from the two horses.

"We are gaining on him!" Sam cried.

But Niall saw Tut throwing things onto the road behind him. Things that exploded with

155

a deafening *BAMM*, leaving holes and craters in Sam's path.

"Look out!" Niall shouted over the deafening racket of the car-sophagus engine.

"I am on top of the case!" Sam spun the wheel this way and that, desperate to avoid the perilous potholes. "So Tut likes to play dirty, eh? Well, so can we!" He pressed a button that displayed a mound with flies buzzing around it. "The car-sophagus has defences: let us now fire hippo plops!"

"Fire *what*?" Niall looked round to find rocket launchers sliding out the vehicle's rear. *FTOOOOM!* Twin brown splats catapulted through the air, high over his head – and sailed straight over Tut's chariot.

"You missed by a mile!" Niall groaned. "It hit the road in front of him!"

"Most true, my friend." Sam winked. "The poop of the hippo is famed for its super-slippy nature . . ."

 157

Suddenly Tut's horses skidded in the smelly slop! One of them did the splits, tripping its neighbour. The jet burners in its butt made it spin over and over, round and round like a giant, neighing Catherine wheel. Tut's chariot went skidding all over the place.

Sam accelerated. "This is our chance to get past him!"

Tut was swerving to and fro, but Sam just managed to overtake.

"Yes! We're winning!" Niall bounced on his stone seat in excitement. "That's well worth a numb bum!"

But Tut pointed a finger at his horses, and in a blinding blur of light they became racing rhinos, thundering along the winding pink road. One of them lowered its head –

159

and rammed its horn into the side of the car-sophagus!

Rocked by the impact, Niall was almost thrown into Sam's lap. "This race is getting nasty."

"I fear it will get nastier," Sam shouted. "Mumbum – rhinos to the rear! Retaliate!"

Mumbum poked his head out of the boot at the front of the car and blasted a thick stream of oil from his nose nozzle. The rhino roared as the goo splashed into its face, and veered aside.

"Well done, boy!" Sam yelled as the car-sophagus pulled away. But moments later –

BOOOOM! Sparks flew from the engine in a cloud of black smoke. "We have blown a fuse!"

Niall clung on as the car-sophagus rocked and lurched. "Let's hope Mumbum can fix it!"

The robo-dog got busy with his screwdrivers and spanners, removing screws and nuts made of gold and stone. He began to woof frantically.

"Try to keep us steady! I'll give Mumbum a hand." Niall scrambled into the back. *BWAMMM!* The car-sophagus hit a huge hole and his head banged against the roof. "Ow!"

161

"Tut is throwing bombs again!" Sam shouted.

A hatch slid open in the roof of the car-sophagus, and Niall poked his head out. Tut's rocket-powered rhinos were close behind, and the boy king himself was hurling missiles. Explosions were going off all around as Sam steered from side to side with sickening speed.

"*Arf!*" Mumbum held an electrical fuse in his jaws, and jabbed it into connecting wires that sprouted from the hole like headless flowers.

Niall took the fuse, reached into the hole and managed to fix the wires in place. "Yes!"

Mumbum started to howl.

"It's OK, boy," Niall told him, "I've fixed it."

The howling grew louder. Niall turned, and cried out in alarm.

Up ahead he saw a gigantic chasm; a split in the red ground as wide as two Grand Canyons and maybe three times as deep. The narrow pink road corkscrewed off into the air, looking more like a rollercoaster than any sort of bridge.

Niall dropped down into the car-sophagus. "What is THAT?"

"A sky-boat launcher!" Sam was gripping

the triangular steering wheel, his eyes wide. "They are used by the flying vessels of KaBa, to help them take off."

"Does this thing fly?"

Sam accelerated. "No."

"No?" Niall felt panic rising. "Then we probably shouldn't drive onto the sky-boat launcher, right?"

"Tut is on our tail!" Sam shouted. Checking in the rearview mirror, Niall saw that it was true. "If we do not take it, he will force us into this abyss!"

"And if we *do* take it . . . ?" Niall realized

that the twisting launch track simply stopped, high in the air. "Oh, seriously?"

Tut's rhinos glowed, and then disappeared in the blink of an eye. At the same time, pyramid-shaped jet thrusters raised his chariot into the air. "My transport can turn into a sky-boat, Mummy!" the boy king bellowed. "Can that silly heap of yours do the same?"

Ka-KRUMMM! The car-sophagus hurtled onto the sky-boat launcher track. Sparks flew off the twisting metal track as six stone wheels bumped and bashed along. The mummy-mobile climbed higher, spiralling into the air; there was

nothing underneath now but gaping, empty space . . . and still Sam drove faster, pushing the engines to breaking point.

Niall pointed ahead, to where the track stopped dead. "We're coming to the end of the line!"

"Let us hope we are going fast enough to reach the other side." Sam gritted his teeth, sweat soaking his bandages. "If not, we will plunge to our doom!"

Chapter Twelve

A Haunting Conclusion!

The end of the launch track came closer . . . closer . . .

Niall shut his eyes, heart thumping. *WHOOOOSH!* His stomach seemed to fall through his trousers as solid ground fell away.

Suddenly the car-sophagus was shooting through space!

"Are we going to make it to the other side?" Niall cried.

"I would like to say yes," said Sam. "But in truth, I cannot!"

Niall opened his eyes – and squeaked. The other side of the chasm was far away, and already the car-sophagus was beginning to drop.

Tut pulled alongside in his flying chariot, a smirk on his face. "I told you I would win this race!"

"The race is not over yet!" Sam shouted back.

Niall felt a bump beneath his feet – and heard

169

a muffled woof. Leaning out of the window, he saw that Mumbum was now underneath the car-sophagus, his jets straining to keep them up. The heavy stone vehicle began to level out. "Good boy, Mumbum!"

But it seemed that the mutt-butt's added paw-power wasn't enough. Still the car-sophagus was dropping . . . Niall watched in horror as a craggy red cliff began to draw nearer.

"We are going to crash!" Sam shouted.

"Yes, you are!" Tut guffawed. "I am the winner – ha ha! I am— *OOOF!*"

A black-and-white blur soared out of the sky, struck King Tut – and knocked him straight out of his chariot! *"AWWWWWK!"*

"That is not an auk," cried Sam triumphantly. "It is an ibis!"

"Lionel!" Niall cheered as the ibis perched on Sam's head and solemnly pecked him on the ear.

"Nooooooo!" Tut yelled, falling through space. "I cannot be harmed. I can control everything from inside the K-Casket . . . and that includes . . . the landscape!"

With a sudden scraping, crunching sound, the chasm closed up! Tut struck the ground and sank in, like a boy-shaped brick plunging into bubblegum. Mumbum and Lionel flew away from the car-sophagus as it landed a moment later, scraping and bumping over the hardening surface until it finally screeched to a halt.

"Ughhhhhh," groaned Niall. "I think my stomach has turned to mush!"

"I'm glad *my* stomach is kept in a jar." Sam climbed unsteadily out of the car-sophagus, scanning the sky.

"Hey! That race didn't count!" Tut was clambering to his feet. "Best of three, OK? *Eek!*" He jumped in surprise as his chariot crashed down beside him. "Wait. Where's the K-Casket . . . ?"

"There it is!" Niall saw it nearing the ground, still in free fall.

Tut reached out, ready to catch it. But Sam shook a scarab beetle from his sleeve and threw it at the boy king's face.

"Ugh!" Tut swiped the beetle away, staggered backwards, and . . .

CLANG! The K-Casket hit a jagged rock.

Niall gasped at the sight of a big dent in the side of the ancient console.

"Noooooo!" Tut put his hands to his face in horror. "You made me miss the K-Casket! If it's been damaged . . ."

Niall frowned at Sam. "Mum and the Snitch and the whole town are caught in there!"

"When Lionel pecked me on the ear, he

whispered to me." Sam looked nervous. "He told me to let the K-Casket crash."

The silver console had started to shake and hum and pulse with light. And all around them the weird KaBa landscape seemed to be pulsing in time with it.

Niall held onto Sam's arm as the ground shook beneath them. "What's going on?"

"You stupid mummy!" Tut was staring around wildly. "The K-Casket's sudden impact has started a *system* crash! The console is shutting down, and out here I can't stop it!"

"Of course!" Sam cried. "At last the K-Casket

will reset itself! And perhaps – just perhaps—"

"Everything else will be reset too!" Niall cried.

Then the world went crazy. Both the sky and the land blurred into pixels, spinning about in a smear of colour. A loud scraping, scrunching sound filled the smoky air, and a whirlwind of colour and light spun through Niall's senses.

The red ground grew green and grassy. The sky became clear and pale, with a single sun shining down. A sphinx went tumbling through the air and disappeared. The distant rows of pyramids puckered and pinched and became

terraced houses. *It's the real world*, thought Niall.
*It's being spat out of the K-Casket – while KaBa goes
Ka-back inside!*

"No!" Tut wailed, rolling about and bang-
ing his fists in a
tantrum as light
and sound swarmed
around him. "This isn't
fair! No one tells King Tut
what to do! I want to stay up. I
want to do whatever I like!"

"No one may do that, young boy king!"
Sam said sadly. "Sometimes we must do what

177

we are told for our own good."

"And it's about three thousand years past your bedtime!" added Niall. "So come on, now . . . GAME OVER!"

Defeated, Tut hung his head and stomped over to the pulsating K-Casket. The second he touched it, he vanished in a lightning flash. Sam and Niall were thrown backwards, tumbling over and over . . .

Until they landed in a bush.

An ordinary, green, leafy, Earth-type bush.

Niall looked around. They were in the park on the other side of town. Some baffled children

were staring at the car-sophagus, parked just in front of the swings. Then Mumbum barked and Lionel flapped about a bit, and the kids ran off.

"It looks . . . normal." Niall turned to Sam. "Is it?"

"I believe so." Sam beamed and applauded Lionel, who landed beside him. "Thank you, great bird of the scrolls! Your crashing wisdom was most wise."

"Yeah, nice one, bird!" Niall grinned. "But can we get back home and check that Mum and the Snitch are all right?"

"Let us go at once." Sam scooped up the

K-Casket in both arms, then pulled aside the bandages over his ribs to reveal a red jewel — his ruby of transportation. "Mumbum, drive Lionel home in the car-sophagus," he commanded as a cloud of ruby smoke began to engulf him.

Niall held onto Sam's coat sleeve. "See you back at Base, guys!"

The world went hazy, and Niall shut his eyes.

When he opened them again, he was back in next door's garden. The fences were standing again. No sphinxes roamed in the long grass.

"Back in two secs!" Heart thumping, Niall scrambled over the fence and ran back to his

own house. He threw open the kitchen door. "Mum? Ellie . . . ?"

They were both in the kitchen, staring at him.

"Where have you been, Niall?" asked his mum.

"Er . . . mainly I've been zipping in and out of an ancient games console built in another world, racing a digital version of King Tut in a stone car that can't fly, and fighting giant sphinxes."

She looked blank. "Whatever are you talking about?"

"Oh, nothing much." Niall shrugged. "How about you two? Any weird memories about being an action hero?"

Ellie tutted. "Niall, you're so immature."

"Whatevs!" Niall turned round and ran back out of the door. "See ya later!"

He climbed the fence to find Mumbum driving the car-sophagus up the garden path; Lionel sat proudly in the boot, preening his feathers. A sliding door in the Pyra-Base wall opened up

automatically to let them in, while Niall made for the main entrance.

"Sam!" he called. "You were right about everything being reset. Mum and Ellie don't remember a thing."

"Really?" Mew came strolling out of the operations room. "I shouldn't be surprised. Human minds are so terribly titchy-small."

"It is well, my friend." Sam emerged behind her, still carrying the K-Casket. "The humans around us will not remember how close they came to disaster."

"What about the ghost of King Tut?" Niall

nodded to the console. "I feel a bit sorry for him. He wasn't really bad – he just wasn't used to not getting his own way."

"Now the console is switched off, his ghost will sleep peacefully once more." Sam patted the dented K-Casket. "And do not worry – I shall not be turning this thing on again in a hurry!"

Niall smiled sadly. "Not even to see a glimpse of KaBa?"

"The Earth is my home now," Sam told him. "And I am here to protect it, no matter what."

"Good for you, bandage-brains! You protect

184

the world, and I'll eat all its fish!" Mew rubbed her wrapped-up tummy. "Mmmm, it is good to be back."

"And it's all because of Lionel," Niall noted as the old ibis waddled into the hallway with Mumbum. "If he hadn't dive-bombed Tut like that, Sam and I would be history, and the K-Casket would never have crashed and reset itself. I think . . . you ought to say thank you."

"Thank you?" Mew almost choked. "To . . . a bird?"

Lionel put his head on one side expectantly.

"Oh . . . very well." Grumbling quietly, the

185

cat goddess bowed her head. Lionel bowed stiffly back and gave a satisfied squawk. Mumbum yapped happily, wagging his bandaged tail.

"Now!" Sam put down the silver pyramid and brushed his hands together. "No more playing of games. Let us return to our business of seeking out villains and bringing them to justice!"

"After a little rest, huh?" Niall looked at him hopefully. "After this *haunting* experience, I'd

like a quiet life for a while."

"A quiet life? With us living next door?" Sam winked. "I am sorry, Niall, my friend – you do not have a ghost of a chance!"

MYSTERIES OF ANCIENT EGYPT

With your wise guide and hostess,

Great Mew!

Hello, good evening and haddock! It is I, Great Mew, back again with more truths for you from the distant past!

FRIEND? FOE? PHARAOH!

The pharaohs were a great bunch really. They were the kings (and queens) of my beloved Egypt.

It was the Ancient Greeks who came up with the word "pharaoh", meaning "great house" – a reference to their royal palaces – and from the New Kingdom onwards (about 2,500 years ago) the name stuck.

So if you liked their pad, you could say, "HEY! GREAT HOUSE, GREAT HOUSE!"

No, boy, you could not!

The kings and queens of Ancient Egypt were very important. They didn't just rule the country, they were seen as special people beloved by the gods and worshipped in a similar way. It was said the pharaoh could communicate with the gods, and part of the job was to please them with rituals, offerings and temples built in their honour.

191

CHARIOT TIME

Since pharaohs were so powerful, they could choose their own entertainment, however grand or expensive – and for many it was racing with chariots.

Lots of people might think that the Ancient Romans came up with chariot races, but no – the Egyptians came up with the idea first!

First and foremost, chariots were used in battle, often as a platform for archers. Then the pharaohs started to use them to ride around in when visiting their subjects. Before long

someone thought it would be a great idea to start having races in them too.

There were some master chariot racers, but rarely did the king take part – which is why young Tutankhamun was so keen to have a go!

Don't we know it!

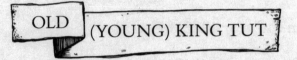
OLD (YOUNG) KING TUT

Tutankhamun became the King of Egypt in 1333 BC at the age of nine. He was not king for long – he died when he was just eighteen – but he (and especially his advisors) brought peace to the country after many arguments over which gods to worship. (While I was arguing over which CODS to worship – MEOWWWWWW!) To please the gods, he also approved the building of many monuments, temples and shrines.

Although history notes he was not a very distinguished ruler, we know lots about him

because, in the year 1922, his tomb was discovered almost completely intact. The riches and relics it contained – over 5,000 items – have told us much about the life of a pharaoh.

The mysterious deaths of some of the people who found Tut's tomb led to many believing that it was cursed. But really, of the fifty-eight people present when the tomb was opened, only eight died over the next twelve years.

Curses!!!

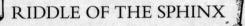

RIDDLE OF THE SPHINX

The sphinx never really lived on Earth – it was a mythical beast with the body of a lion and the head of a man. The famous Sphinx at Giza in Egypt is the world's largest statue carved from a single piece of rock. Many believe it was built around 4,500 years ago, created to act as a guardian of the pyramid complex of King Khafre.

'Sphinx' is actually the Greek name for these statues. We do not know for sure what the Egyptians called them, because nothing was written down.

Me?
I call them
SCARY!

On that, Mummy, we can agree! Now, I feel a fish-feast coming on, so until we meet again – FAREWELL!

Great Mew would like to thank the human Ancient Egypt Advisor Louise Ellis-Barrett for her help with this section.

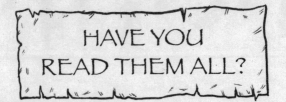

HAVE YOU READ THEM ALL?

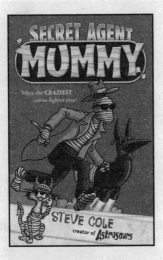

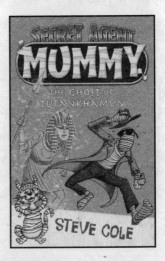